A NOTE TO PARENTS

Reading Aloud with Your Child

Research shows that reading books aloud is the single most valuable support parents can provide in helping children learn to read.

- Be a ham! The more enthusiasm you display, the more your child will enjoy the book.
- Run your finger underneath the words as you read to signal that the print carries the story.
- Leave time for examining the illustrations more closely; encourage your child to find things in the pictures.
- Invite your youngster to join in whenever there's a repeated phrase in the text.
- Link up events in the book with similar events in your child's life.
- If your child asks a question, stop and answer it. The book can be a means to learning more about your child's thoughts.

Listening to Your Child Read Aloud

The support of your attention and praise is absolutely crucial to your child's continuing efforts to learn to read.

- If your child is learning to read and asks for a word, give it immediately so that the meaning of the story is not interrupted. DO NOT ask your child to sound out the word.
- On the other hand, if your child initiates the act of sounding out, don't intervene.
- If your child is reading along and makes what is called a miscue, listen for the sense of the miscue. If the word "road" is substituted for the word "street," for instance, no meaning is lost. Don't stop the reading for a correction.
- If the miscue makes no sense (for example, "horse" for "house"), ask your child to reread the sentence because you're not sure you understand what's just been read.
- Above all else, enjoy your child's growing command of print and make sure you give lots of praise. *You are your child's first teacher—and the most important one. Praise from you is critical for further risk-taking and learning.*

—Priscilla Lynch
Ph.D., New York University
Educational Consultant

D0042585

To Rachel and Joey
— G.M.

Text copyright © 1994 by Grace Maccarone.
Illustrations copyright © 1994 by Meredith Johnson.
All rights reserved. Published by Scholastic Inc.
HELLO READER! and CARTWHEEL BOOKS
are registered trademarks of Scholastic Inc.

Library of Congress Cataloging-in-Publication Data

Maccarone, Grace.
    Soccer game!/ by Grace Maccarone : illustrated by Meredith Johnson.
        p.   cm. — (Hello reader)
    Summary: Brief rhyming text follows a group of children through
some exciting plays during a soccer game.
    ISBN 0-590-48369-2
    [1.   Soccer — Fiction.   2.   Stories in rhyme.]   I. Johnson,
Meredith, ill.   II. Title.   III. Series.
    PZ8.3.M127So   1994
[E] —dc20   93-43742
                                                                        CIP
                                                                         AC
21 20 19 18 17 16   7 8 9/9

Printed in the U.S.A.   23

First Scholastic printing, August 1994

SOCCER GAME!

by Grace Maccarone
Illustrated by Meredith Johnson

Hello Reader! — Level 1

SCHOLASTIC INC.
New York Toronto London Auckland Sydney

We start the game.

We're ready.

We aim.

We pass.

We fall.

They get the ball.

Away they go!

We're doomed!
Oh, no!

It's in the air.

Our goalie is there!

We dribble.

We pass.

We slip
on the grass.

We kick. We run.

We're having fun!

We see a hole.

We run to the goal.

The ball goes in.

Hooray! We win!